Dear Reader,

Books have the power to fuel our imaginations and open our hearts. *Moira's Birthday* is an uplifting tale of a young girl who invites her entire school to her sixth birthday party, despite her parents only allowing six kids.

This beloved story by Robert Munsch is a Canadian classic. *Moira's Birthday* teaches the importance of togetherness, collaboration, and inclusion—important principles, especially at a time when our friendships feel and look different than before. Through its vivid scenarios, engaging illustrations, and heartwarming messages, *Moira's Birthday* is bound to draw in readers of all ages.

As part of our continued efforts to support children's literacy programs, TD and the Canadian Children's Book Centre are thrilled to present a copy of this classic book to every Grade One student across Canada.

We are proud to mark the 20th anniversary of the TD Grade One Book Giveaway. In the past two decades, we've distributed more than ten million books to first-grade students nationwide.

I hope this is one of the many great books you and your family share to continue your love of reading.

Have fun and enjoy *Moira's Birthday*!

Bharat Masrani
Group President and CEO
TD Bank Group

For more information on all TD-supported reading initiatives, see tdreads.com

Dear Reader,

The Canadian Children's Book Centre (CCBC) believes that celebrating Canadian stories is so important. We are thrilled that *Moira's Birthday*, written by Robert Munsch and illustrated by Michael Martchenko, is the 2020 TD Grade One Book Giveaway title. As we celebrate 20 years of the TD Grade One Book Giveaway, we are reminded of the way books can bring us together as a community. *Moira's Birthday* joins 19 other phenomenal picture books that have been selected as giveaway titles since 2000.

Working with ministries of education, school boards, and library organizations, the CCBC distributes over 550,000 giveaway books each year. With so many uncertainties in our current world, one of the few things that we can be sure of is the power of stories to heal, to make us laugh, and to foster a sense of connection with each other. It is exciting to be able to introduce this Canadian children's favourite to a whole new generation of young readers who will fall in love with this joyful story.

For additional information, resources, and programs promoting reading, visit **bookcentre.ca**.

Happy reading!

Rose Vespa
Executive Director
The Canadian Children's Book Centre

The Canadian Children's Book Centre

Moira's Birthday

STORY by
ROBERT MUNSCH

ART by
MICHAEL MARTCHENKO

annick
press
toronto • berkeley

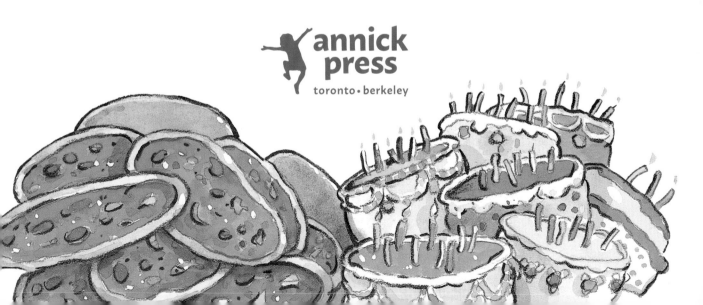

One day Moira went to her mother and said, "For my birthday I want to invite grade 1, grade 2, grade 3, grade 4, grade 5, grade 6, aaaaand kindergarten."

Her mother said, "Are you crazy? That's too many kids!"

So Moira went to her father and said, "For my birthday I want to invite grade 1, grade 2, grade 3, grade 4, grade 5, grade 6, aaaaand kindergarten."

Her father said, "Are you crazy? That's too many kids. For your birthday you can invite six kids, just six: 1-2-3-4-5-6; and NNNNNO kindergarten!"

So Moira went to school and invited six kids, but a friend who had not been invited came up and said, "Oh, Moira, couldn't I please, **PLEASE, PLEEEASE COME TO YOUR BIRTHDAY PARTY?**"

Moira said, "**UMMMMMM . . . OK.**"

By the end of the day Moira had invited grade 1, grade 2, grade 3, grade 4, grade 5, grade 6, aaaaand kindergarten. But she didn't tell her mother and father. She was afraid they might get upset.

On the day of the party someone knocked at the door: rap, rap, rap, rap, rap, rap. Moira opened it up and saw six kids.
Her father said, "That's it, six kids. Now we can start the party."

Moira said, "Well, let's wait just one minute."

So they waited one minute and something knocked on the door like this: BLAM, BLAM, BLAM, BLAM.

The father and mother opened the door and they saw grade 1, grade 2, grade 3, grade 4, grade 5, grade 6, aaaaand kindergarten. The kids ran in right over the father and mother.

When the father and mother got up off the floor, they saw: kids in the basement, kids in the living room, kids in the kitchen, kids in the bedrooms, kids in the bathroom, and kids on the **ROOF!**

They said, "Moira, how are we going to feed all these kids?"

Moira said, "Don't worry, I know what to do."

She went to the telephone and called a place that made pizzas. She said, "To my house please send two hundred pizzas."

The lady at the restaurant yelled,

"TWO HUNDRED PIZZAS! ARE YOU CRAZY? TWO HUNDRED PIZZAS IS TOO MANY PIZZAS."

"Well, that is what I want," said Moira.

"We'll send ten," said the lady. "Just ten, ten is all we can send right now." Then she hung up.

Then Moira called a bakery. She said, "To my house please send two hundred birthday cakes."

The man at the bakery yelled,

"TWO HUNDRED BIRTHDAY CAKES! ARE YOU CRAZY? THAT IS TOO MANY BIRTHDAY CAKES."

"Well, that is what I want," said Moira.

"We'll send ten," said the man. "Just ten, ten is all we can send right now." Then he hung up.

So a great big truck came and poured just ten pizzas into Moira's front yard. Another truck came and poured just ten birthday cakes into Moira's front yard. The kids looked at that pile of stuff and they all yelled, "**FOOD!**"

They opened their mouths as wide as they could and ate up all the pizzas and birthday cakes in just five seconds. Then they all yelled, "**MORE FOOD!**"

"Uh-oh," said the mother. "We need lots more food or there's not going to be a party at all. Who can get us more food, fast?"

The two hundred kids yelled, "**WE WILL!**" and ran out the door.

Moira waited for one hour, two hours, and three hours.

"They're not coming back," said the mother.

"They're not coming back," said the father.

"Wait and see," said Moira.

Then something knocked at the door, like this:
BLAM, BLAM, BLAM, BLAM.

The mother and father opened it up and the two hundred kids ran in carrying all sorts of food. There was fried goat, rolled oats, burnt toast, and artichokes; old cheese, baked fleas, boiled bats, and beans. There was eggnog, pork sog, simmered soup, and hot dogs; jam jars, dinosaurs, chocolate bars, and stew.

The two hundred kids ate the food in just ten minutes. When they finished eating, everyone gave Moira their presents. Moira looked around and saw presents in the bedrooms, presents in the bathroom, and presents on the roof.

"Uh-oh," said Moira. "The whole house is full of presents. Even I can't use that many presents."

"And who," asked the father, "is going to clean
  up the mess?"

"I have an idea," said Moira, and she yelled,
"Anybody who helps to clean up gets to take
  home a present."

The two hundred kids cleaned up the house in just five minutes. Then each kid took a present and went out the door.

"Whew," said the mother. "I'm glad that's over."

"Whew," said the father. "I'm glad that's over."

"Uh-oh," said Moira. "I think I hear a truck."

A great big dump truck came and poured one hundred and ninety pizzas into Moira's front yard. The driver said, "Here's the rest of your pizzas."

Then another dump truck came and poured one hundred and ninety birthday cakes into Moira's front yard. The driver said, "Here's the rest of your birthday cakes."

"How," said the father, "are we going to get rid of all this food?"

"That's easy," said Moira. "We'll just have to do it again tomorrow and have another birthday party! Let's invite grade 1, grade 2, grade 3, grade 4, grade 5, grade 6, aaaaaaand kindergarten."

THE END

To Moira Green

Special edition prepared for the TD Grade One Book Giveaway Program.

This edition is published by special arrangement with the Canadian Children's Book Centre and TD Bank Group for free distribution to Grade One children across Canada.

Text copyright © 2020 Bob Munsch Enterprises Ltd.
Illustration copyright © 2020 Michael Martchenko

Originally published in 1987 and 2019 by Annick Press.

The Canadian Children's Book Centre
Suite 200, 425 Adelaide Street West
Toronto, Ontario M5V 3C1
www.bookcentre.ca

Annick Press
Suite 200, 388 Carlaw Avenue
Toronto, Ontario M4M 2T4
www.annickpress.com

Printed and bound in Canada by Friesens Corporation
Also available in French: *L'anniversaire*
ISBN (English) 978-1-988325-10-1
ISBN (French) 978-1-988325-11-8

Library and Archives Canada Cataloguing in Publication
Title: Moira's birthday / Robert Munsch ; illustrations by Michael Martchenko.
Names: Munsch, Robert N., 1945- author. | Martchenko, Michael, illustrator. | Canadian Children's
  Book Centre, issuing body.
Description: Originally published: Toronto : Annick Press, 1987. | "This edition is published by
  special arrangement with the Canadian Children's Book Centre and TD Bank Group for free
  distribution to grade one children across Canada."
Identifiers: Canadiana 20200298380 | ISBN 9781988325101 (softcover)
Classification: LCC PS8576.U575 M56 2020 | DDC jC813/.54—dc23